UNSPEAKABLE

DANIEL DAVIS WOOD is a novelist and essayist based in the Scottish Borders. His début novel, *Blood and Bone*, won the 2014 Viva La Novella Prize in his native Australia, and his follow-up, *At the Edge of the Solid World*, was published in 2020. He is currently at work on a collection of essays on literature, culture, and philosophy.

UNSPEAKABLE

Daniel Davis Wood

ThisIsSplice.co.uk

First

1

TWO YEARS AFTER the last time we spoke, an old friend of mine was convicted of having committed a terrible crime. The news came to me from a mutual friend with whom I'd also lost contact. The three of us once shared a flat on the Meadows until a hike in rent and rates pushed us onto separate paths. I'd long since skipped town altogether, but Lindsay, I learned, had managed to make a new home for herself. Now the proud owner of a bedsit in Leith, somewhere close to the water's edge, she told me as much as she'd heard of the things that Noah was said to have done. She set it all down in a long email and sent it to me with links to the verdict and the proceedings and a dozen reliable news reports written at various points in the process.

In a photograph embedded in the text of one report, Noah sat despondent in the dock. He bowed his head with eyes askance, a tension to his pallored lips. A shadow curled in a sunken cheek as he turned to avoid the camera's flash. The crime had occurred as the dregs of autumn darkened into a savage winter. With ten days of police enquiries followed by fourteen in court, Christmas was only a fortnight away and the polar winds were howling. The court was preparing to recess, according to what Lindsay wrote, while Noah remained behind bars awaiting delivery of his sentence.

2

WHEN I THINK BACK NOW on my response to Lindsay's news of Noah, I'm sure I left her unsettled by an apparent failure to care. Here's the truth, though. I'd just returned home exhausted after back-to-back shifts at two different jobs when I found her message in my inbox. I bent over my computer and read the things she wrote about Noah and in an instant I felt numbed, robbed of all action, unable to piece together even a disjointed reply with questions or denials or crude expressions of revulsion and disgust. Noah's crime had muted me before I could find any words to address it, and so, with no notion of what to say, I never replied to Lindsay at all. I offered her only silence, enigmatic and resolute, which I know I would have despised, would have denounced as unforgivable, if somehow our places had been reversed and she had offered that silence to me. In my thoughts I envisioned her baffled, pacing between her bed and her laptop while waiting for my outrage to burst across her screen. But what Lindsay couldn't see was the chaos beneath my inertia. Just the first few words of her message unleashed in my mind a rampage of memories, replays of all my exchanges with Noah back in the days when we three shared a single roof.

Noah and I had bonded as strangers in a strange land. We met as far-flung expatriates in a pub on the Bruntsfield Links. We noticed we shared an accent and learnt we shared a hometown as well, and soon enough we realised we were connected by degrees. I had friends who had friends who lived near his parents in Oxley.

He had a cousin who'd gone to my school and finished a year after me. Bit by bit we exchanged anecdotes from our lives back home in Brisbane. Day by day we shared notes on how to survive being new to Britain. Had he said anything to me then that held no meaning the first time I heard it but might, in hindsight, have hinted that he was capable of doing what he'd recently done? How much of the monster he'd now become was already there when we forged a friendship? Had that monster shared my house, had it shared my company, nestled somewhere deep inside him, hidden from the wider world, like a parasite patiently gorging itself into the fullness of its being? He'd once returned home from work with the news that he'd been abruptly reassigned, transferred from customer service to a desk that denied him public contact. He once said he had an uncle he loathed for reasons he wouldn't divulge, and in passing he'd mentioned to me that he no longer spoke to his younger sister. He'd once admitted, too, that what led him to move abroad, to start afresh in Scotland, was an urge to put himself at a distance from some disturbance back in Queensland and, with luck, to find himself a wife and settle down.

Only briefly did I meet the woman to whom he'd been engaged. Dour, demure, and nine years his junior, Iliya came from Russia but longed to live in the west, and she'd flown over to stay for a weekend, once, to see if Scotland could meet her hopes. I remember distinctly the way her tears welled up as she prepared to fly home and await a decision on her residence permit. Beyond that, though, I recall nothing more than the night the four of us shared a meal and Noah told the story of how he and she had met. Candlelight bathed his face as he spoke. Wine gave life to his words. Chance had drawn them together, he said, one night in a lodge in Tralee. He'd been close to the end of a year spent skirting the coastlands of Europe. She was scouting out new attractions for a travel agency in Omsk. She'd been sitting alone beside a fire when he asked if he might join her, and with those words he sparked a discussion that didn't end until daybreak.

When I heard this, I remember, I felt myself swept up in the romance of their union. Could it really have been so simple, so nearly predestined, as he suggested? Could two total strangers fall in love so suddenly that marriage plans would be in place before they'd known each other a week? Only when Noah's story returned to me later did I start to wonder about the things he'd probably elided. Iliya's longing to live in the west must have enticed her to accept whatever lifeline he might throw her. A wife made submissive by the threat of deportation must have seemed to Noah to be worth a considerable cost. As melodramatic as I know it sounds—which is perhaps one more symptom of my shock—my view of Noah underwent revision so that, in retrospect, he became for me a pitiless spider snaring a fly. I saw how he'd spun bonds around the vulnerabilities of his victims, selecting his prey from those too trusting to detect his malice; and so, from my fading memories of his wife, I felt my thoughts swerve towards the one he'd most recently seized. I surprised myself when I saw that they hadn't earlier taken this turn. I suppose that the crime and my knowledge of the criminal had led me to trace out the lines of his web, but that in doing so I'd blurred my own view of the people he'd managed to trap in it.

3

THE REAL NAME OF NOAH'S VICTIM was never released to the public. I now know what it is but I'm not able to disclose it. As soon as she tumbled into my mind, I returned to the reports I'd received from Lindsay in search of clues to the girl's condition. What scant clues I came across only hinted at her existence. I leapt from one report to the next, printed them out until they covered my floor, sat on the hardwood to read and reread them, and then I read through them again. Drawn in by dissatisfaction, sensing some vital absence, I felt my curiosity fuelled by the lack of the disclosures I'd hoped would feed it. Estimated periods of recovery, ranging from ten days to more than two weeks, were circumscribed by subtle redactions of all other details of the girl's wellbeing. Of course the nature of the crime made her situation sensitive. Only so much could be said before the limits of what could be said would be breached. Although she'd clearly been looked upon as a subject of urgent discussion, the girl was also somehow taboo and not to be discussed directly. From page to page, report to report, a fog of unsaying occluded her. Reading on, reading again, reading between the lines as closely as I could, I fought to retrieve her from this fog and I forced myself to feel for her at least some scraps of sympathy until, suddenly spent, I stopped. I stopped because I had to. The whole thing left me exhausted. Time and again I'd lunged after a shade that vanished upon the slightest approach.

What came next was anger, anger that simmered into a rage, as I saw how the words that evoked the girl turned against her to conceal her, to reduce her to a plaything waved about to pique the public interest. It was then, in the heat of this rage, that I thought back over all those reports and felt my floundering sympathies reach out for someone else, some other person in her story. Each report made passing mention of the victim's father. He was, I learnt, a respected member of his local community, admired by many for deeds that were yet undefined. Despite the lack of further details, I allowed my thoughts to dwell on him and I saw that the two of us shared a subtle sort of kinship. In my mind's eye he took form as a man of discomposure. Long limbs and ungainly height, and a restless, nervous energy. Tufts of thinning hair, a face creased with frown lines and crow's feet. I fancied that this man, whoever he was, was out there somewhere engaged in business much like mine. Perhaps bent over an oldtimer's bar, nursing a bottle of whisky, or perhaps alone and sober at home in a room of dim light and shadows, he too must have been led by rage to scour his memories of Noah in search of any strangeness he should've questioned when he had the chance. My own behaviour struck me as a resonance of his, and so I supposed I might know the troubles that plagued his mind. Shame burns through my body, of course, upwards from heart to head, when I put these thoughts into words and see them here in black and white. They strike me now as audacious at best and, at worst, arrogant beyond excusing. Even so, in the moment, they were the thoughts I entertained and the thoughts I acted on. Despite the distance between us, despite our having never met, I felt close to the father of that nameless girl and I felt a powerful need to feel closer still. I tamped down whatever sparks of shame might have sprung up inside me and I hurled myself at the mess of thoughts I'd thought would be his.

If I was that girl's father, I thought, I could not now direct my thoughts to Noah without craving violence. I envisioned myself as that man, that father, beating the blood from Noah's face, capillaries bursting around his eyes, crimson snot slung over my knuckles, using the very same hands that had earlier stroked the hair of the girl in her hospital bed. I imagined that all my love for the child would simply dissolve into fury at Noah, I suffered the inexpressible rage that just the sight of him would provoke, and then I withdrew from the other man's mind to imagine the two of us as friends so that I might stand beside him, rest a supportive hand on his shoulder, and quietly offer encouragement for whatever vengeance he planned to pursue. But I mention these details only to show how my own turmoil distorted what I thought I knew of him. It clouded my vision with misapprehensions that real life quickly corrected. I later learnt that what made this man so prominent in his community was his service as fulltime rector of his family's parish church. He delivered sermons and provided counsel and conducted various ceremonies, and his reputation for doing these things upended what I'd assumed of his response to Noah's crime. Violence now seemed to me beyond his capabilities. Vengeance contravened the dictates of his moral code. His heart might have beaten with rage at the monster, but suddenly I became certain that it would never compel him to beat at the face of the monster itself. The hands with which he might have punched and pummelled Noah would only ever be clasped and wrung together anxiously, or else offered to others in dutiful gestures of comfort.

The first time those hands touched the girl in the wake of her ordeal was when he embraced her outside their home in the taut air of a wintery dusk. He stood in the garden awaiting her while her mother parked the car in the driveway. He stepped forward and opened the passenger door, moved aside while she climbed out, and then with a weak but welcoming smile he put his arms around her, kissed her on the cheek, and whispered some words about feeling better now that she was home. But how must it have really felt to embrace her there, right *there*, beside the neighbouring terrace? Only a month or so beforehand, he and she had watched their new neighbours haul an entire household indoors under the threat of a downpour. Stormclouds had blackened the sky. Raindrops had pecked at the pavement. Overhead thunder had promised a deluge and distant lightning, drawing nearer, demanded faster movements. The fridge and the sofa, rushed inside, were followed by bookshelves, a dozen or more, and then came the private library crammed into fifty or sixty cartons.

When I try now to picture Noah's face as the girl and her father would have first seen it, eyes alert but nose and mouth obscured by the boxes he held in his arms, I see that he must have appeared to them much as he appears to me these days. Every so often when I go out, and more so since I did come across him, I glimpse certain details of passing faces that for a moment convince me I have seen him in the flesh. Those faces are never actually his, just a fringe and brow and a sharp gaze over a low wall or the top of a newspaper, but when they catch my eye at an angle I can't avoid extrapolating from them to recreate the rest of his features. All I need to be certain I've seen him again are those few attributes glimpsed by the girl and her father when he entered their lives.

What I learnt, eventually, was that the man whose thoughts I hoped to know had stood there awaiting his daughter's return after having made no visit to her on the hospital ward. I can't imagine he took his absence lightly, especially for a man with his daily occupations, and I sense it came less from an empty heart than from the trauma of his failure to protect her. I *couldn't* do it, I hear him murmur to his wife on the night of their daughter's discharge. He sits opposite her without looking at her, a man shrunken down to a wraith in an armchair too rigid for him to relax. The listlessness in his tone shows his wife the distance that divides him from the man he used to be. She has just spent twelve days at the bedside of the wounded girl, the girl safe again in her own bed on the other side of a nearby wall, and she listens to her husband confess the pain that lances his tortured soul. I pulled myself together, he says, I got ready to visit, I showered and dressed and every day I walked out the door but when it came down to *actually* leaving—

He cuts his words and draws a breath before his defences devolve into babbles and whines.

The shock of what Noah did to his daughter had shackled him to the seat of his car. I sat there, he says when he manages to calm himself once more, I sat at the wheel and I turned over the engine, again and again, and then I got out and I came back inside and I sat here in this chair. I knew what I had to do. I knew what I *wanted* to do. I wanted to go and see her, hold her, say something to comfort her, but to actually stand and leave this house to do those things—

He drops his gaze to the ground and rakes his fingers back through strands of grey.

I didn't have the will, he says. So I didn't, couldn't, go.

He'd been the one, after all, to reach out and welcome the new neighbours into his home. He'd been on his way to work when he'd seen her, Noah's wife, standing outside on her stoop the morning after moving in. During their light conversation, as I have come to picture it, he noticed her rest a gentle hand on a belly beginning to bulge with new life, and I'm sure this was why he asked if she and her husband would join his family for dinner. They arrived near dark with a knock at the door. The girl in her bedroom heard her father entreat them to step inside. Refuge from the chill. Radiators humming. Warm amber light on the living room walls, the cold air confined to the corners.

While wine flowed freely around the table, as I know it did, I suppose the girl sat down in silence and watched the adults laugh and drink, and I'm told that her awkwardness there among them was what led Noah to catch her eye.

Wan flames wavered atop the last few stubs of wax. Crumbs lay scattered across a tablecloth blotched with droplets of red. Clinks of spoons against bowls of strawberries filled a lull in the conversation and then, to break the silent spell, to cast a spell of his own, Noah leant across to the girl and, in a mock aside, in a loud theatrical whisper, he posed an unpredictable question for her alone to answer but for everyone to hear.

Is there any chance, he asked her, that you have a fondness for poetry?

Although he arched an eyebrow as if expecting an instant reply, his words refused to wait for the girl to respond. He leapt to his feet, drunk on high spirits, and with a smile he launched into recitation. Nonsense verse that no-one could place. Something obscure from his graduate years. The vibrancy of his performance overwhelmed all other chatter. He rose from his chair and ambled around with sing-song rolling off his tongue and brought levity to the table. I'm told that the girl was especially beaming. I'm told that he had her entranced, enchanted. I'm told that with this performance put on for her pleasure, he shone a spotlight in her direction and saved her from being lost in the thick of the adult world. Now, though, I hear her father lament, she's just one of those kids they tell you about each night on the news. I see the man sitting at home in company of his silent wife. He scratches his scalp, behind his ear, and shifts his weight to one side of his chair. He runs his tongue over chapped lips and stares into vacant space. I used to have a daughter, he admits to his wife with a sigh, but now I feel I have only some girl who someone made a victim.

4

THE GIRL'S MOTHER sped her to hospital as soon as she stumbled upon her. At first, I've been told, the victim awoke to find the woman at her bedside. A friendly face amid the glowing graphs that monitored her vitals. Warm hands on her hands, a voice of calm and comfort, and with them both a sense of incipient reassurance. Then the victim suffered a procession of doctors and counsellors and policemen asking questions, endless questions, investigating this and that. The victim refused every meal she was offered and had to be force-fed through tubes that gagged her. The victim could not even see her own face until three days had passed and the swelling had subsided a little. She raised the mirror someone gave her and winced and felt the wincing hurt. A face beyond recognition snarled and squinted with blackened eyes. Smashed and crooked rows of teeth robbed her of her speech. A bandage held fast to her broken wrist and padding encased her aching bones, and somewhere, I'm sure, she felt the heat of stitches clasping together a wound still rough and raw.

All she'd wanted to do, as far as I can tell, was return a borrowed book to the man who'd lent it to her. When Noah's performance had come to an end he'd told her she could read it and he'd darted across to the neighbouring terrace to retrieve it. A book of poems, he'd whispered as he handed it to her, and later that night, before he went home, she'd been lying on her bed, immersed in the volume, when he'd approached to say farewell. I see him in the doorway as a shadowed form backlit by light from elsewhere in the house. I hear him shift with a sound that captures her attention, and I see her whip around to fix her eyes upon him. Assuming he must have come to ask her to return his book, she rises from bed and moves to him with the volume in hand. I see her shrouded in coy pyjamas, only minutes away from lights-out, with balloons of blue and gold coasting across her stomach and chest and up and down her arms and legs. Did she catch his gaze sweeping over her, rising from bare feet on carpet to take in her ankles, her thighs and waist, her chest and shoulders? Her collarbone protruded beneath taut white skin. Her pale pink lips drew down in a pout. Her auburn hair cascaded over the nape of her neck and dangled in front of her brow in strands whose shadows hid her eyes.

The girl offered Noah the book and offered awkward thanks for it.

Keep it as long as you like, he said. He forced a smile at her and added, Just hand it back whenever you're done.

She was done by the following Friday and set out to return it that morning. She left the house before she was even ready for school. The transcripts of the trial reveal that she stepped outside barefoot and wearing the same ballooned pyjamas she wore to bed each night. Apparently when she glanced out her window she'd seen Noah's car exhausting smoke with its engine idling in the driveway. Apparently Noah had set it running to fend off the biting cold of the snow that had fallen overnight. On a moment's impulse, then, the girl had deduced that he was still home and dashed to the neighbouring terrace to find the door wide open. From someplace she wasn't able to see, through the hallway bisecting the house, the airflow carried the kick of burnt toast. A tentative knock at the threshold. No immediate response. The girl wiped her feet on a bristled mat and took a step inside. She paused a moment to call out a greeting and then a muted voice gave way to footsteps and Noah stepped into sight. He held a mug of steaming coffee. The girl extended the book for him to take with his free hand.

Finished? he asked as he reclaimed it. You can borrow another, if you want.

He turned and gestured for her to follow. She found herself trailing him down the hallway and into an open-plan kitchen. On the benchtops and on a table and on the floor around her feet, books lay strewn about and stacked together and thrown haphazardly into boxes. I remember the mayhem of all those books. I remember how they'd very nearly owned the flat I shared with Noah. I remember, too, how just a hint of interest in them would elicit generosity. Feel free to read whatever you like. That's what he'd say whenever he noticed anyone browsing the covers and spines. I'm sure that's what he said to the girl when he saw her gawping at them. Feel free to read whatever you like, just let me know what catches your fancy. He retreated down the hallway and disappeared from view as she thanked him and set about examining his trove. But I'm told that over the following days, struggling to answer the questions put to her in hospital, she never was able to say exactly how he came to be holding her by the wrist.

Confusion must have flourished between them in the house. Perhaps she tried to find him to thank him again for the loan or to show him which new titles she'd selected. Perhaps he'd vanished into the hidden spaces of his home or darted outside to turn over his engine for better defence against the cold. Apparently, as she searched for him, she'd found the door to the bathroom open and seen herself reflected in the head-and-shoulders mirror within. Apparently, acting on impulses that escape my understanding, she'd entered the bathroom and drawn close to the mirror to peer at the image it cast and that was when Noah came to her. He confessed at trial that he'd spent some moments by the door to linger and watch her watching herself. She'd opened her mouth to bare her teeth and even poked out her tongue, he said, and then she'd stood on tiptoes and turned side-on to see her reflection from the waist up. She drew a breath and puffed her chest, sucked in her stomach, puckered her cheeks, and then with a sense of human presence she startled and spun to find Noah behind her. At that stage, as I understand it, there was something amiss with her hair. Faint strands swayed in a breath of wind that ghosted in through the open front door. For just a moment she turned back to the mirror and gathered her hair in a ponytail. Someone at school had told her she'd look better if she wore it that way. He told the court she'd told him this and he said he'd agreed. Then he'd rested one hand on her shoulder and raised the other to hold the ponytail for her. How she felt when he did this, tense or ill at ease or something else entirely, I'm not able to say because I can't even guess. She must have let her hair drop then, to let her hand fall to her side, but as she released it she also must have felt it brush over her shoulders and neck. Her hand remained behind her head where his hand held it fast. He tightened his grip around her wrist with fingers tensed against her veins. She found she could move her own fingers but could not move her arm. She must have tried to speak, must have stammered some protest, but must have done so without effect because at that point something snapped.

How would it have unfolded from there? Before she could have known what had happened she probably felt hot tears down her cheeks and perhaps even heard someone shriek. Fabric ripped, cast aside: coloured balloons thrown over the tiles. Cold air clutched at her toes and thighs and pawed at the small of her back. Her hand, I imagine, slipped into the bathtub and blasted out a trombone blare. She said she tried to grab something steady, felt herself falling, struggled to stand, fell at last. She said she saw tiles, a drain, the ceiling and the ceiling light and then tangled pipes beneath the sink, until she felt herself overturned and felt her face against the floor. Her hair blazed like fire in front of her eyes. Her lungs swelled up as if to burst and her heart pounded blood so hard it threatened to blow a hole through her chest. Inside her there was movement as he moved against her and then her teeth moved back and moved around in her mouth. She split her lips when her face smashed the sink. The porcelain grinding into her gums gave her her tortured grimace. Her left eye pulsed with pain as well, blackening into a bruise as tears pooled in the socket. Finally, when the ordeal was over, she collapsed with a slap on the floor. All she could hear, she later said, was heavy breathing not her own. All she could smell was sweat, she said, and all she could feel was the pain that would afflict her for days to come.

Those were the days during which her father did not bring her comfort. I wonder if she overheard his excuses the night of the day she went home again. I wonder if she lay in bed, awake and alert in the dark, and heard him unburden himself to his wife on the other side of the wall. I couldn't, he says, I couldn't do it, I couldn't leave this house, I couldn't. The girl, I imagine, goes rigid when her father's confession reaches her ears. I couldn't do it, she hears him murmur, I couldn't go, and she hears him trying hard to hold himself together simply by repeating those words over and over until he can't say anything more. His words fragment and fall away into senseless heaves of air, the jagged breaths of a man who can no longer contain the anguish that scalds him like acid inside.

He had good reason to feel that anguish and he has it even now. He couldn't have known, would not have dared suspect, that the trial would end with such a whimper. I learnt about it when I read the reports I received from Lindsay, tracing the course of the courtroom arguments until they reached their grim conclusion. The prosecutors appealed to the humanity of the jury. They played with emotions and pulled at heartstrings and pressured the jurors to imagine themselves in the place of the traumatised girl. But the defence didn't counter the charges in hopes of winning Noah's freedom. His lawyers vied only for a show of leniency in the sentencing. They dodged the question of accountability and asked instead for due respect to be paid to Noah's character. They dismissed the morality of the charges against him to speak of a submission to awful impulses. They attributed his crime to a fleeting lapse of control from a man who had strived for years to accrue a reputation for integrity.

After he and I had parted ways, I learnt, he'd patched together a career as a fledgling intellectual, a tutor and lecturer at half-a-dozen colleges across the county. His lawyers defined him as a scholar in the making, a dedicated teacher, a loving husband who would soon become a proud and devoted father, tragically born with a flaw in his soul and upstanding enough to not deny it. What they meant by what they said was that his crime was not his fault. What they did was portray him as a man so enslaved to his passions that he was, in a sense, imprisoned already. The man was of course summoned at trial to speak in his own defence. Yet when the time came to account for his actions, he not only made no denials but made no attempt even to explain. He offered only a meagre apology, a token show of remorse, in what one report described as a choking voice through which the slightest glint of humanity tempered the inhumanity of his crime. He was sentenced to nine years in prison before he could apply for parole. He wouldn't be a free man again at least until the girl was a woman. Even so, he'd be released almost as soon as the law said her girlhood was over.

5

I'VE OFTEN WONDERED what a sentence so weak did to the girl and her parents when they heard it handed down. I imagine her father and mother alone, together in darkness sometime after dinner, staring intensely at empty plates as the verdict bedevils them. I imagine mumbled complaints about the judge, cursory vows that they'll launch an appeal. But I imagine, too, conflicted feelings about the prospect of further legal pursuits. Although the girl's father must have craved some harsher retribution, he also must have felt averse to the torment of a second trial, and all the more so because the first had tormented him least of all. His wife had suffered more than he'd done; she'd *seen* the injured girl, she'd seen the damage with her own eyes, and for that reason she, too, had been summoned to the stand. She testified, distraught, through tears that flowed without relent. She wiped at her eyes with the back of a hand and smeared her tears across scarlet cheeks. When she raised her voice to speak directly into the microphone, her words went suddenly weak and she had to speak in a rasp.

She spoke of how she'd woken that morning to find her daughter not in bed, not inside the house at all. She'd taken a glance outside, noticed footprints in the snow, followed them where they led to the neighbouring terrace with its door still open. She spoke of her rising concern and then of explosive panic. She called out for Iliya, she called for Noah, she strained as hard as she could to listen for a response, and that was when she caught the shudders of someone, somewhere, weeping. When she came to the bathroom, she said, she found blood across the ground and found her daughter covered in it. The girl's hands were stained the colour of rust. She curled into herself like an injured animal helpless beneath the sink. At that sight the woman felt a plummet in her heart. The girl tried to pull her torn pyjamas down over her thighs, down to her knees or even her toes, but then a voice struggled for something to say and the woman became aware of someone else in the room.

Iliya sat on the edge of the bathtub. Tears streaked her face and enflamed her eyes.

The other woman stood at the door with a stillness that urged Iliya to speak.

She wouldn't let me touch her, Iliya said without lifting her gaze from the girl. But, she went on, she's hurt so bad, I couldn't leave her here alone.

Iliya said the same thing to the jurors when she was called to testify, and said it again to me when we spoke just before she left the country. She told me much more than that as well. She told me about the trial and its aftermath, and she gave me the details I'd sought in the reports that left so much unsaid. Of the girl or her mother she knew almost nothing, but she said she'd heard that the sentence brought the girl's father to breaking point. Lost his faith, lost his job, left his wife, lost his mind. She told me this in a torrent of words that belonged to a woman very different from the waif I'd encountered years beforehand. She told me the story as best she remembered, she said, the way she'd originally heard it when she sat down to confront the man with whom she'd hoped to share a life.

At first, she revealed, Noah flat-out refused to receive any visitors. Only after the authorities prevailed upon him did he finally relent. One fine day in his first year behind bars, he sat behind a glass barricade while the girl's father stood and waited for him on the other side. The glass captured and mirrored the ruined man's features and overlaid them on the face of the monster he sought to confront. He'd fled his church that morning with resentment throbbing so powerfully through him that he couldn't care any longer if the building stood abandoned. His wife had always sworn she'd divorce him if he quit. I'm told that that was the first thing he decided to share with Noah. His job, he said, had been the reason he'd uprooted his family to move north in the first place. What would it mean for his life if he were to give up his work? As he spoke he refused to let his gaze settle upon the prisoner. Then he stood and ruminated on all the things he might yet say before he resolved to speak at greater length.

I was the only one who wanted to leave Kent, he said. But I was blessed to have married a woman who'd sacrifice her wants to help me achieve my dream. But it's a pathetic dream now, anyway, isn't it? To rise every Sunday and address a congregation and have people come to me as their friend and confidant and unburden themselves on me and place in me their, their *faith*, and to have them trust me to be there for them in times of need and promise them that all will be well and God forgives them for whatever they've done, and on and on, on and on—

He threw his hands in the air and banished the emptiness from his eyes and he glared down at the man sitting silent behind the glass.

The glare was a defence, of course, as he sought to conceal from Noah the confusion he can't hide from me in my thoughts. Questions harrowed his brow. Why even bother with this life? Why go on with it at this juncture? Why preach hope when you lose your own faith in the very thing on which you have founded your being? Why advance the word of a God who won't protect the family of so devout and devoted a servant?

I wonder if Noah could sense the outrage rising in the other man. I wonder if he saw the agony in the scowl, the flare of nostrils, the clench of fist and flex of fingers. Perhaps a flicker of fury did indeed colour the other man's expression, or perhaps its being written here has less to do with reality than with my reading of him. Nevertheless, some signal of his inner state must have shone through clearly enough to move Noah to speak in turn.

I'm told that he offered a simple apology and that this was what triggered the tirade. You don't *need* to say you're sorry! That's what the other man spat at him. You feel regret for your actions, I know. Some days you're consumed by it. This doesn't come as news to me. It's what I expect of a man behind bars. But what *sort* of regret do you feel? I don't think it's anything even *close* to remorse. It's severe enough to compel you to beg my forgiveness, I'm sure, but not out of deep regret for having broken a moral limit. Only out of frustration with the consequences you've incurred. So, of course, when I hear you mutter your worthless little apology I can't help but wonder. Do you apologise because you're *genuinely* sorry for what you've done to the people I love, for having blown our lives to pieces? Or do you apologise out of fear that if you and I were alone together I might try to harm you, *punish* you, so that your most urgent desire right now would be to say or do something drastic to push me out the door?

Noah had no chance to speak before the other man pressed on. I used to have a daughter, he said, but she's dead to me now because you killed her. She's lost, an enigma, tangled up in the mess you scribbled over her. He raised both hands in front of himself, palms upturned in a gesture of hopelessness, and then he let flow a stream of furious accusations, *infection* and *corruption* and *pollution* and *perversion* and worse words that vanished into the air only when his tongue tripped and he tumbled into speechlessness. He chewed at his lip and stared at Noah, and stared at Noah, until the sudden slam of a hand rattled the glass in its pane. What followed was a stillness in which he disappeared into the depths of himself. What musings came to him in that room? I wonder if he wondered, then or at some other stage, what might have happened, what he might have done, if his daughter's ordeal had hurtled towards its most intractable conclusion. I wonder if he'd wondered which horror would have been the more awful, a newborn child brought into the world or otherwise denied the chance, and whether he would have been strong enough to help his daughter cope with either trauma. He must have wondered, he couldn't have helped it, and I'm sure that all his wondering went with everything else inside him into the slap at the glass that left the blur of his handprint stuck, suspended, between him and his adversary.

What troubles me most right now, however, as I dwell on what I know of this scene, is a question that began to trouble me when I first learnt of their encounter. It can only have troubled Noah as well from the instant he sat and peered through the glass and watched the girl's father lingering, lost, on the other side. Why exactly had he come? What could possibly be his agenda? What did he hope to achieve with his presence? The heartache that drew the man into the room could have been no mystery, but mystery shrouded whatever he thought he might take away with him. The mystery hovered somewhere around him, able to be sensed but not to be perceived, until once again the girl's father drew breath and set forth to say something more.

Speak, he commanded. Speak to me now. He didn't glare at Noah, didn't even glance at him, but let his eyes wander over the glass without gazing through it. Speak, he said. Speak to me, will you? Open your mouth and say her name. Say her name, Noah, he said, and with those words he said the name he'd promised himself he'd never say. Say her name, he said, say her name to yourself and make her a human being.

Only after he said this much did his eyes meet Noah's. Then he whispered a question that I know he asked although I cannot say exactly how he meant to pose it.

Make her a human being, he said. Can you begin to do that?

Perhaps he meant it as an honest request, perhaps he laced it with spite. Perhaps he intended to put to Noah a challenge that would haunt him with uncertainties about his innermost nature. But a consequence of its being asked is that it haunts me here as well and leaves me to wonder, to really wonder, if Noah was at all able to do what that man asked of him. How could he begin to humanise that girl? How could he have been capable of it? How could he make himself see a human being, a true and living soul, where before he'd seen only a body lacking every human quality more immanent than flesh?

Whether Noah, when he spoke, demanded to know the point of this exercise or only bluntly registered his visitor's distress, I can't say for certain. I never thought to question Iliya on the outcome of the other man's approach. It's possible, if I'm to be honest, that I just didn't want to know any details beyond the ones she volunteered. In my version of events, in my speculations on how things unfolded, Noah did not speak aloud the name of the girl because he wasn't able to force himself to the task. On some level I guess I must have wanted him to not be able to speak and, as I write these words now, I suppose I still want him to be unable, to be unable forever and always. As I see it, he simply sat there and watched the other man flee, abandoning him to solitude in the emptiness of that room. There, I hope, Noah heard in his head the name he'd elected to not utter, heard it echo inside him, and tensed up as it lodged itself deep in the conscience he thought he could barricade against it.

Later

6

A LITTLE BIT MORE THAN a decade went by between the events I have detailed so far and the first time I felt the need to coerce them into words. The contours of my life are sufficient to set the scene. Illness, recovery, relapse. Something inside me went haywire and took a long time to heal. Then emigration, once, twice, the first time on my own, the second time with a partner, and finally a third upheaval, more illness and another flight from life, and once again I found myself alone. I stumbled on for more than a year before I'd regained enough strength to start rebuilding. The fallout sent me back to the last place I'd felt like someone real. I wanted to reclaim a sense of self I worried I'd lost forever.

That's how I returned to Edinburgh ten years after leaving. I felt more or less as adrift as the first time I saw the city, but even so, and even in the teeth of another ferocious winter, the place seemed to me like a refuge, a shelter on a citywide scale. I set aside some time to properly convalesce, to do whatever I had to do to keep a relapse at bay. But because my limited means left me with nowhere to live for long, I ended up on the sofa of someone I used to sleep with, and because her limited means didn't allow her to heat her flat, I took to rising early each day and wandering the streets in search of cheap coffee and respite from the cold. Then one morning in January, as a numbing gale assaulted the city, I strayed into Waverley Station, up the stairs from the platforms and into the mezzanine food court, and there I caught an unmistakable glimpse of the features I thought I glimpsed all the time.

A decade's difference had thinned his hair and worked worry-lines into his brow. His lips had drawn and his shoulders rounded, and he wore a shade of stubble across his cheeks and chin. Even so, there was no denying that those features belonged to the person I knew and not some stranger with similar looks. He stood behind a countertop that shimmered with shocking light. He braced himself with both hands gripping the service bench. He wore an apron uncomfortably over a uniform starched bright white, and pinned to his lapel was a red plastic tag that broadcast his name in big bold letters for all the world to see.

Without a pause I sat at a table and watched him from afar. He spent a long time idling there and drifting off into thought. He straightened piles of napkins, he refilled a box of straws. Occasionally, sporadically, customers appeared and spurred him to act. A herd of teenage boys pressed him for a round of milkshakes. An old lady out on the town ordered a boxful of donuts. As I watched him I found myself flexing my fists, pressing my palms against the matte of the tabletop. I didn't know at all what to think of seeing him in front of me. Should I rise and speak to him? Should I stay seated, hold back and observe?

Until I found my thoughts in a jumble, I hadn't realised I'd made assumptions about how he'd be living now that he was free. I'd assumed he wouldn't have stayed in Scotland after he'd been released. In fact I'd assumed he'd be ordered to vacate the country for good. I thought he'd run home to Queensland, like me, to hide away and lick his wounds. I even remembered convincing myself that we'd crossed paths in Fortitude Valley a month or so before I escaped Australia again. Standing in the doorway of a café on Brunswick Street, I could've sworn I saw his face through the window of a bus stuck in traffic. But here I was and there he was, each of us still on the far side of the world, brought together once more, despite my assumptions about his fate, on the far side of a decade as well.

All morning I sat at the table, unmoving, and watched him perform his work. At lunchtime he made a hot dog and ate it in two bites. Then he whipped up a smoothie and slurped it down in less than a minute. He swept the floor of the service area and swiftly cleaned the coffee machine, and neatened a basket of croissants and pastries gone stale throughout the day. I went on watching, on towards dusk, until he reached the end of his shift. Approached at five by a thin young woman no more than eighteen or nineteen years old, he was relieved of his duty and he readied himself to go. He gathered up a beanie and wrapped a scarf around his neck. As he walked off he slipped into a coat whose hem fell past his knees.

What I did next was in no way something I had planned to do, but as soon as he started to leave I knew I couldn't let him leave alone. I felt no desire to follow him or to know where he was living. I felt no compulsion to find out where he went after work or what sort of life he'd made for himself. I felt not the slightest need to fill in the gaps in his story and learn his reasons for staying in town instead of starting again elsewhere. And yet, though I can't account for it, some outward pressure made me set off after him. I suppose I felt moved by some vague sense of duty, some responsibility to his fate, issuing straight from the shock of having been there in his presence. I felt obliged to follow him much as I might feel the need to seek the source of a strange noise in my house. I felt as if the world had pushed him back onto my path for a purpose, compelling me to understand his return before I would be free to continue on my way.

Downstairs, outside, into the wet of an early dusk. I walked behind Noah at a distance of about a city block. We headed towards the Haymarket as the last of the sun pierced the clouds overhead. I crossed the sheen on the wet cement and felt my cheeks scorched by the wind behind the rain. As dark set in I followed Noah briskly along Dalry Road. The tyres of passing traffic swished spray onto the pavement. The downpour strobed through the beams of rushing cars, and puddles in gutters soaked commuters stepping out to hail buses. Finally rounding a corner and then edging around another, where streetlights laid glowing arches across the stones of a cobbled road, I came to a block of terraces with a bus shelter next to the footpath. I paused and let Noah walk on a little. I watched him flip the latch on a gate outside one of the houses. When he swung the gate open I dashed through the rain to slip inside the shelter. Noah halted at the gate to unlock a postbox beside it. He reached into the box and removed a paper that ruffled in the rain and stuck to the back of his hand. He peeled it from his skin and stood to read it in the dim light, and he fell into a sudden stillness that set my mind to wandering. Whatever that paper might have said, it kept him too long in the cold.

I suppose I should say I'm ashamed to admit that I saw it as vigilante propaganda. The truth is that I wasn't ashamed to see it that way at the time. I wanted Noah to hesitate because he'd been immobilised, because with a spotlight shone upon him he'd been frozen by the fear of having his ugliness exposed. I pictured a pamphlet that named him and gave a name to his crime in enormous print. Beneath the tabloid headline lurked a grotesque caricature. Two beady eyes peered through a gap in a hedge where bony clawed fingers parted the leaves beside a white picket fence. The new address of the criminal sat beside details of his crime and his sentence. What followed from there was a declaration that the people have a right to know, to be informed when a man like Noah attempts to settle where parents are raising their children. Summed up in only three sentence fragments, sketched out in the broadest of brushstrokes, his life became something larger than life and made public for all to condemn.

He shuffled towards his door, unlocked it, clicked it closed behind him. His absence robbed me of anything to focus on except the shadows that washed across the front of his terrace. In one sense, that's where this story ends. There were, there are, no further events for me to record or report. In another sense, though, it was exactly the threat of that ending that led me to refuse it. Despite his departure, I couldn't leave. I continued to stand where I'd sought refuge in the shelter. I continued to keep my eyes on his house. I felt a more disquieting fantasy at the edges of my vision, and as I stood there I allowed myself to focus on its unfolding.

7

The ease of the afternoon's escapade had thrown me into a trance. The ease of slipping unnoticed into Noah's new life. The ease of coming across him out there by happenstance and then, without betraying my presence, returning with him to where he'd resettled. Why, I wondered, should all that be so easy for me and not just as easy for anyone else? If I could do what I'd done, I thought, then surely the girl who would now be a woman could follow in my footsteps. If she ever saw him out there, if she ever chanced upon him in public, if she ever managed to trail him through the city streets as well, then what? How painfully would her shadowing of him rupture whatever life she was living? What would her life have even looked like at that moment?

As these and similar questions started to plague me, alone in the dark, I watched her walk into view beside me and stand nearby like a stranger awaiting the 6.26 to Princes Street. She moved with a stiffened gait, with her face fixed against expression. Far too thin with thin red hair and freckled cheeks flecked with rain, she made no sound, none whatsoever, and stood and stared at Noah's house with a gaze that gave no hint of feeling. Then, with that image of her standing by my side, summoned into existence by me, I led my thoughts towards more realistic questions. If she ever saw Noah in public and felt inclined to follow him, could she actually do it, one foot in front of the other, or would she not be able? And if she could, could she then do what I could not and make her way through the dark to his door? And even if she could do that, forcing her feet up those steps, could she bring herself to knock, to announce her presence to him, and then await his answer no matter what form it might take?

I don't know this girl, this woman, whoever and wherever she may be today. Intellectually, of course, I'm aware that I have no right to subject her to speculations, nor any real justification for having done so then or after the fact. All the same, I can't deny the wanderings of my mind. I conjured her up from thin air and projected her onto my world. Those are facts I can't write around. My suspicion is that she would have fallen into fantasy, too, if it ever came to actually knocking. The knock would have drawn out her sense of passing time. It would have stretched the space between the lowering of her hand and the turning of the handle on the other side. In that brief eternity, her mind would have spun with all the things she thought he might say when he stood there looking out at the street and saw her suddenly in front of him. He'd wrench open the door and tell her she didn't need to knock because he heard her heavy breathing as she gambolled up the path. He'd glare into her eyes and command her to leave straight away because the restraining order prohibited him from being anywhere close to her. He'd stare at his feet or at her feet, or at an empty spot on the ground, and he'd find himself unable to say anything to her at all.

But no, none of these things would happen because really it would unfold in no way she could imagine. First a tired shuffle from somewhere deep inside the house. Then the squeak of metal on metal, a peephole cover pulled aside, the paralysed pause of a man only inches away and sweltering in thoughts he cannot calm and order. Nothing would happen for some time until the creak of the door and complaint of a hinge would open up clear air between them. The first thing the woman would see, however, wouldn't be his face. He'd steady himself at the threshold where the cold would grip his bare arms and there she'd watch a whiteness pinch at the flush of his skin.

What next? What then? What's truly unknowable is not whether she might arrive at his door but whether she might step through it at his invitation. I can't believe she'd ever really put herself inside his house, but standing with her in the shadows I felt I needed her to do it and so, obediently, she did. Noah held open the door and asked if she'd like to come out of the cold. Some reflexive sense of courtesy? Some drive towards self-flagellation? I watched him turn and retreat down a hallway while, once again, she trailed him at a distance. Then he moved aside, stepped into his living room, and waited for her to follow his lead. When she entered he gestured towards a lonely single-seater in the corner. She folded her arms across her chest and abruptly turned from him. She rejected the only offer he was capable of making. He blushed from throat to temples and pressed the heel of a hand to his forehead, and he took the seat for himself with a slump of resignation.

He sat precisely where I placed him, where I wanted him to sit, and felt his further humiliations alive in the surrounding space. How dark and dank the hovel he had taken as his home. Kitchen and laundry both in one room. A sink stacked full of dirty dishes and cupboards stocked with readymade meals. Boxes of books atop one another, lined against walls bereft of shelves. His name tag remained fastened in place on his lurid lapel, boldly announcing to her who he was as if she wouldn't know him by his face. He must have felt these humiliations because I wanted him to feel them, and why, after all, shouldn't I want him to feel them and try my best to make him feel? Think on what he did to that woman. He did more than break her body with his brutal force. He broke her capacity to be seen by others for who she was, to be *herself*. He reduced her, for me, to a means to an end, an instrument to be snatched up and used to strike at him. He flayed her into a crude abstraction lacking form, a host of weightless words through which I might torment him with what he inflicted on her, even though I know those torments will not leave a scar. She was once a human being, a living, breathing person, but he stripped her of her humanity in more eyes than his own. Now I find I'm not able to see it. I can't know enough of her self to bring her to life on the page. Worst of all, I can't shake the feeling that I am finally just like him because I, too, cannot do otherwise than use her for my purposes.

So it is that her wandering eyes alight on the first thing to light up my mind. A picture, framed, atop a table. A pale boy with shiny black hair and a heartwarming smile. Probably no picture like that ever occupied any such place, but certainly the boy in it occupies my thoughts. At first, as I see it, Noah says nothing of what the young woman has noticed. He simply hopes her eyes will roam past it. But they don't. Instead, they fixate on it. Eventually they have halted there so long that he feels compelled to explain. So, then, he speaks to her, and in speaking he retreats into memories he'd otherwise not revisit.

My son, he mutters. My son. Then he mutters a name I miss before he chokes his words with a cough.

8

THE LAST TIME Noah saw his son was the very first time they ever met. The glass barrier made his whole body ache to be on the other side. The ache pinched his face into a cringe he had to strain to conceal. Watching the boy through the glass he must have wanted nothing so much as to reach across and touch him and know, at last, the feel of him and the scent and to hold him in his arms. For Noah the meeting ended five years of only imagining the boy, five years of knowing no more than the facts of his name and date of birth and physical features conveyed in others' words. What he couldn't have known at the time was that the meeting would also usher in yet more years of isolation.

Hard plastic chairs, a slot in the barrier for a parcel to be pushed through. A present. It was or had recently been the boy's birthday. Noah chose to give a book, of course, but he chose a title he should've suspected would be too demanding for someone so young. Call it a stark reminder of his displacement from everyday life. Then his efforts to lighten the mood with chit-chat only heightened the dislocation the boy already clearly felt. What grade are you going into at school? What's your favourite subject to study? What do you like to do on weekends? These were the sorts of questions he posed, bewildered and superficial, and in return the boy offered only bewildered and superficial replies.

When Noah found he could probe no further, he let his questions fill the air until, in a move to dispel a silence, he asked the boy where he and his mother were living now. He didn't need the name of a street or a suburb or even a city. In the hills. By the sea. Simple descriptions would be enough. But the boy turned around in his seat to face his mother where she sat behind him. With a shake of her head she killed all hope of a bond between father and son. The rest of their conversation dragged on to the ticking of the clock and came to an end, at the top of the hour, as the boy and his mother switched places.

Iliya told me all this herself when I heard from her much later, entirely out of the blue. By that stage a couple of years had elapsed since I thought I'd seen Noah pass by me in Brisbane. That sighting had spurred me to try to contact her, to reach out and reconnect, but nothing came of my efforts and I was quick to give up hope. Then, unexpectedly, she sent me an email, asked me for my number, wondered if we could talk. She said she wanted to tie up some loose ends. She said she'd gone to see Noah in prison only a couple of days earlier, and now she wanted those who knew him to know what she'd said to him and why. I gave her my number, my time, my attention. I didn't expect to find in her the kindred spirit she turned out to be. I've taken care to record what she told me as faithfully as I can recall it, not least because what she went on to say, what she went on to do to Noah with words, feels to me like an echo of the impulse that drives me to say all of this.

She stood before him with poise and command, her hair drawn back severely and her posture tense. Then she took her seat and made herself the centre of the room.

Noah thanked her, respectfully, for bringing his son to visit him.

A flick of her hand told him she wouldn't waste time on petty pleasantries.

Honestly, he whispered with a wince, I've told you I'm sorry, haven't I? I'm so sorry for all of this, for everything I've done. I'm sorry and I'm sorry and I've said it a thousand times but I'll say it once more if that's what you need me to do. I'm sorry. How many apologies do you want me to give? What more can I possibly say?

No, she told me she said. She remembered clearly how she laid bare her nerves by answering his questions with this blunt *non sequitur*. Don't, she went on. I'm done with apologies. I'm here with you now only because I want something else from you.

Really, she said when I spoke to her later, I wanted to see him again for one reason. I wanted to see him so I could say something to *hurt* him.

At the police station where he'd initially been held, before he'd been questioned with his lawyer in the room, she'd ridiculed him by playing dumb and pleading with him to insist on his innocence. They sat together, he in handcuffs, in a room with concrete walls and a bar heater that struggled to combat the cold. She leant back in a seat a constable had offered her and waited for the constable to leave before she spoke. Her rounded belly had started to show in the fifth month of her pregnancy. The constable closed the door behind him. Now she turned her eyes to Noah.

Tell me you didn't do it, she said. Tell me they made a mistake.

He did as she asked and held himself together to prove the truth of the words he'd utter. I'll be out in no time, he said. All it is is they got the wrong guy.

So she told him she'd been in the bathroom to see for herself the damage she knew he'd caused. Yet in spite of her admission, he wouldn't drop the façade she'd asked him to assume.

It's no mistake, she told me she told him as he grew more insistent. I know what I saw and I know what you did, so please just come clean and tell me the truth. I know what it is but I know I can't rest until I hear you speak it.

Still he pressed on with rote denials and without any waver in his voice. All it is is a mix-up, he said. I told you before, they've got the wrong guy. Whatever it was they were saying he'd done, she said he said he didn't do it. Even as she turned aside and left him to sit by himself behind bars, he didn't seem able to force any more truthful words from his mouth.

He must have known, he *must* have known, how false his words would sound to her. In the bathroom of the house he knew she'd have to return to, a stockpile of forensic equipment would put the lie to his claims. And when she'd seen the girl's mother break down at the sight of the child on the floor, she'd had to summon the strength to call the police and point them in Noah's direction. Even if she couldn't be certain that he was responsible for the savagery, she also couldn't have seen many other possibilities. Only half an hour had passed since she'd run to the shops to feed a craving. Noah had been there when she left the house and he was gone when she returned. His hasty departure all but announced his guilt. What must it have cost her then to alert the police to his crime? What effort to take the phone in hand and speak the words that would ruin her? And what price did she continue to pay? She'd feel her husband's deeds returning vividly to life whenever she entered that room again to brush her teeth or wash her hair or draw herself a bath, and her nights would be lost to sleeplessness in a bed left cold by his absence. Even so, when she spoke to him afterwards, he still would not speak to what she knew of his deeds. He talked and talked and talked, she said, but what he said was nothing.

She told me she'd had to brace herself before she could say what she'd said to hurt him. She had to brace herself even for me when I asked her to repeat it. Creases at the corners of her mouth were not quite concealed by the hair she let hang to her jawline. Her weathered face went blank and her eyes, exhausted, emptied. After the birth of their son, she said, she'd succumbed to postnatal depression. Her days started bleeding together, dissolving into a senseless haze with no escape in sight, and having admitted this to Noah she lashed him with revelations. Every time she was pulled out of sleep by bawling, every time she blew her budget on clothes and food and toys, every time she lost hours at work because the boy required care at home, she felt the urge to just leave her child behind and abandon the life her husband had forced upon her. Her immigrant status denied her any substantive support from her family, and Noah's defence costs had robbed her of all their meagre savings. She said she'd often wondered what value there was in living like this, from day to day. Suicide beckoned, she admitted, it beckoned more than once, until she somehow tapped a new reserve of fortitude. She said she couldn't say exactly how the changes came about, but gradually she came to feel that she, of all people, might make amends for the things her husband had done to that girl.

I confess I don't understand her logic, even after long reflection. I concede that's likely because her logic isn't explicable so much as purely emotional. It had to do with justice, she said, with striking a moral balance. If Noah had ruined the life of a child, she might make recompense for him by doing her best to struggle on and raise one. But to find the resolve for that to happen, her son, their son, could have no hope of ever being close to his father. She'd whispered all this to her husband in jail with the boy sitting there behind her, and she'd asked if Noah could see the sense in what she was trying to say. If you weren't locked up in here, she said, I would never have felt so strongly about the need to not fail our son and I would've just spiralled down to disaster. I'm alive and I'm here beside him only because you went away, because I felt for him a sense of total responsibility that couldn't have been mine to feel if you had not been absent. What makes this boy so perfect now is the care I've given him to compensate for your *cruelty*. But take a good, long look at him here, she said as she sat before Noah, because when I take him out of this room I will take him forever out of your life.

Of course he protested that she and the boy could visit whenever they wanted.

She cut him off and told him they couldn't because she intended to move away.

Those words threw weight on his shoulders and sank him where he sat. You're moving? he said. How far? To where?

Abroad, she said. It's paid for. We'll be gone in less than a week.

He'd protested again, she told me later, until she stressed that she held exclusive custody over the boy. At that he began to beg, to entreat, blathering to her about his visit from the father of the girl, the grief he'd seen in the other man's eyes, the consideration he'd given all the things that were said to him, but she told me she spoke over his pleading and told him she hadn't finished what she'd set out to say. He shut himself up with a pained expression and watched her raise her hand and flash her wedding band at him.

By that stage she'd had the divorce papers with her for more than a year, she said, but when she'd first received them she found she'd lost the will to sign. He didn't understand, she told me, and he'd stared at her, dumbfounded, until she made her intentions explicit.

Even if I find love again, she'd said, or if you find it when you walk free, I will never in this lifetime sign my name on the dotted line. I will never sign, she said, because I will *never* divorce you. Our marriage will last as long as we live because, she added as she stood and saw realisation sweep over his face, because I want a splinter stuck beneath your skin.

He shook his head in hopelessness. Just to hurt me? he said. That's your reason?

Just so, she told me. She wanted to hurt him, that was all, so she'd done what she could to cause him pain. His crime had hollowed out their marriage. She would keep him encased in its husk to prevent him ever recovering from his own betrayal of their bond.

She farewelled him with only a nod of the head which opened a flood of grovelling. She guided their son away in silence, exacting and patient in all her movements, and quietly revelled in her revenge for what he'd done to the future he'd stolen from her.

9

WHAT TURNS MUST NOAH have taken through the years, to move from that seat behind the glass to the armchair in that house in Dalry? Swerves along a narrow path with no leeway for deviation. Good behaviour most of the time. Parole and release as fore-ordained. The dole and a place in the jobseeker's queue. The drudgery of a pointless job, regular contact with the authorities who'd promised to monitor him to his grave. What I'd seen in the food court was an aching and decrepit wretch, a transient thing so wearied by the world that he seemed to want to fade away and forsake it altogether. But as I lingered outside his home and thought of him as he actually was, and as I imagined that young woman standing to watch him take his seat, the powers that coerced the two of them into this confrontation faltered and froze the scene.

It seemed improbable, impossible, that those two people could ever come together to converse in peace. The sort of silence that would beg forth words from others yielded nothing, as I saw it, between the man and woman in that room. There were no courtesies or curiosities or casual updates on personal progress that either of them could coax from their tongues. And as I prolonged the time I imagined them spending together, I recognised, inside myself, a burning irritation, a vexation, born from my awareness that their exchange must remain unresolved. It grew in me as I thought on their lives without hope of ever knowing any fixed or certain thing about them, and as soon as I felt it and knew what it was, I felt that Noah would feel it as well when he looked across at his visitor. It was what he'd received from her father, from the irresolute words with which the other man had taken his leave. Make her a human being, he'd commanded. Can you begin to do that? The question, the unanswered question. It opened a vacuum never to be filled. It called out for an answer that lay beyond it. And when the woman at the heart of it came forward to confront him like this, how could the question fail to prompt further words from Noah?

I know you wonder, he whispered to her despite being driven by a failure of knowing. I know you must wonder, he said anyway, if it will ever be possible for you to say, perhaps, that you forgive me. He kept his eyes fixed on a point, a stain, on the armrest of his chair. You must wonder about that, right? he mumbled. You must wonder because I wonder. I wonder about it often. I can't help it, really. It's the people, other people, that set me off, set me thinking. People on the streets, for instance, gathered in cafés or pubs, a park, maybe a food court.

Although he had to have suspected that she followed him home from some public place, these last words did not draw from her the response he surely hoped for.

These people set me off, he said, I guess because they seem so free. They're not like us, you and me. They're not like us at all. Here we are, caught up in this thing, this history, that even now determines every second of my life, and yet when I walk out the door and see all those people I can't pass a single one who has the slightest awareness of it. Something like this, this thing between us, is *everything* to me, but it's nothing, it's trivial, it's nothing at all, to everyone else out there.

He sighed and closed his eyes.

The woman, as I saw her, turned aside from the burbling beast. Actually, then, she also turned aside from me. Who was she, exactly? How could I possibly say? I had, I have, no proximity to her, no access, no way of getting close. Certainly not directly, and not obliquely through other people. Noah's actions obstruct my view. Her father remains too distant, too far removed from her private turmoil. Iliya told me only things she'd heard secondhand, and the newspapers effectively excised the girl from the story of her own life. I'm left to look at her strictly from the periphery of events, and yet what I want is to see her so clearly that she might look back and see me as well. Shouldn't she have a chance to know that someone out there would look upon her not as prey, not as a victim, not as a locus for outpourings of grief, but just as a person deserving of understanding? Instead she grows blurry, becomes opaque, recedes into her own space, encased in the history of all the things that have been done to her.

She stands almost frozen in Noah's presence. What she sees is frost in the corners of windows facing onto the street, and headlights illuminating the sprinkle of rain on the glass. At last, after some minutes slip by, Noah's voice returns to him and sends a shock through the silent room. I guess his story remains the only one that can really be told.

Maybe five minutes, he mutters with no further movement.

As the woman turns back to him, I force her and I force myself to focus on his face and watch him quake while he speaks.

Five minutes, he says again with eyes shut tight and a voice that flinches in frustration. He nods gently until he is satisfied that she knows what he means to relive.

He'd fled his house in a stupor and left the front door open. He'd slipped inside his idling car and felt an inferno engulf him. He'd thrust out a hand to turn off the heater and only then noticed blood on his skin. The car lurched ahead. It lunged to a halt. The grass nearby was brown where melting snow had slushed. Thin mist whitened the Meadows and blurred the public toilets across the way. Harsh light glared across the dull steel walls inside. A tap banged on with force. Icy water turned his fingers a bruising shade and shrink-wrapped skin around veins and knuckles. He massaged first one hand and then the other and finding no soap he scrubbed so hard he broke the flesh. Blood flowed quickly and mixed with the blood he'd gone there to wash away. It waltzed together with the water and swivelled down the drain.

When he returned to the outside world he still mimed the washing of hands. Hand over hand over hand, squeezing and tensing to pressure the wound he'd opened. He moved through the slush to his car. He reached forward to yank at the door. He stopped at the sight of his reflection in the rearview. He peered at himself, as closely as possible, but the glass was so fogged that he couldn't see his eyes. His exhalations steamed across the surface. Until he saw the steam, he said, he hadn't realised he'd been breathing so hard. That's one of the things he told the judge when it came time for him to take the stand.

Now, he went on, all he held on to were vague recollections of clambering up to the podium and spreading out a jumble of notes on the lectern. Students later approached by police said he'd launched into his lesson midway through a sentence and shut up when he'd seen detectives at the door. He said he could feel his shirt stick to his skin where sweat had soaked the fabric. When asked to step aside, he said, he'd heard his own protests booming around him. The microphone pinned to his collar gave them volume for his audience. Finally he'd relented and did as commanded and swallowed the impulse to speak out and defend himself. He'd hunkered into his jacket and cast his eyes to the ground. The murmur that flowed through the crowd crescendoed when firm hands gripped his shoulders to lead him out of the lecture hall and he'd buckled under his shame.

Maybe just five minutes, he mumbled to her again while I stood outside and watched. That's all it took for things to change. Five minutes and maybe not even that. How easy it is to reduce an entire life to ruins. How suddenly the whole thing can be blasted to rubble. With one hand raised, he shielded his eyes to hide from her his welling tears. It was nothing, he said to her softly, nothing, it was nothing. A quick fix, an instant release, that's all. It was impulse, that's all, really that's all. That's all it was, and look, just look, what it did to us.

Of course, it didn't have to be that way. He chose to make it so. He chose violence, he chose to attack, and although I'm sure I'll never understand why, there's no part of me that doubts he knew what he was doing and knew that it would destroy them both.

She looked down at him sitting there beneath her, trying his best not to tremble, but the trembling only quickened until he could not stop himself from breaking apart.

His composure cracked with his voice. As he slouched in his chair, his hair fell forward over his eyes. Then his mouth contorted and ran ridges down his face. When he wept his bottom lip quivered and splotches of red spread over his cheeks. Strings of saliva dangled from his chin until he brushed them away and they clung to the back of his hand. He let out a jabbering cry that was something close to a howl. Perhaps, of course, this is too perverse, this zeroing in on the details of a pain that is only speculative anyway, just to prolong it and deepen it for my own satisfaction. But I can't deny that it captured me as I stood beneath the shelter, as rain cast static over the city and I listened to his stammering. Please, I imagined he said, I'm sorry. Please, he said, if I say I'm sorry will you say you accept my apology? Will you just say something now? I don't care what it is. Talk to me please. Just speak. Even if you've got nothing to say, it doesn't matter anymore. Even if your words are empty, please just say them anyway and I can believe they're not empty at all. And so he went on speaking like this, not to convey any meaning, only to make a noise, and begging that woman to make a noise as meaningless as his.

She didn't because she couldn't because I would not allow it. She stood and watched him wordlessly, her face adamant and gaunted by shadows, while Noah sputtered on towards total incoherence. Please, he muttered, please just, please, and choked out whatever words I gave him and fought off the silence that might have allowed her to do what he implored. That was when I realised just how much I despised him, and, too, I realised that my hatred arose from what he did to me just then. I hadn't seen him for more than a decade and yet I still felt a duty to use my thoughts to torture him, to desecrate my memories of him. Not only for what he did to that girl, not even mostly for what he had done, but simply for having done something so beyond my comprehension that I couldn't help but fixate on it and strive to understand it, even to internalise it, in a way that made me resent him and made me spite him even more.

My narcissism is clear, I know, because of course the distress of Noah's victim belittles whatever discomfort I might feel. But my own sufferings, no matter how facile, are what I have to live and contend with, so they are the only ones of which I'm able to speak truly. I hated him for afflicting me with them. I hated him for having stolen so much of my time, for having exhausted my emotional resources, for having caused me to waste my energies on him and for not being able to banish him from his residence in my mind. I hated him for the fact that I possessed no greater means of doing harm to him than some illusory version of the girl he ruined, simplified beyond all plausibility. Most grating of all is that I still saw her so firmly in the terms he cast her in, I couldn't even envision for her an exit from his stifling room. She flickered out of my sight like a picture on a television unplugged without warning. Her disappearance from his house forced me to exit the scene as well and cast me into the cold again. I hated him even more for that, for denying me any chance of offering her a resolution, and so I went on helplessly tending to my bile.

10

AT LAST I lifted my eyes from the gutters to watch the rain streak through the night air. I backed up against the bus shelter wall to avoid the spatter at my feet. I felt in the hurried beat of my heart an urgent need to leave at once and spring through the rain and leap towards Noah's door and thump on it or kick it in. I wanted to confront him for his deeds and for all he'd done to the people around him. I wanted to berate him, to brutalise him, for everything, for all of it, for concealing his secret self from me when I shared a flat with him, for having emerged as a different person to the one I thought I knew. I wanted to beat him, to break him, and to do it all for my own pleasure as well as on behalf of those who I knew would dream of it but would be too timid to risk it themselves. But of course I suppressed my wants as well, forced myself to quell my spite, and closing my eyes I listened awhile to the rhythmic gushes of distant wheels slicing through water on asphalt.

The dark, the rain, the senses sparked by standing there alone: so much inertia, even now, and so much embroidery on my stasis. I watched Noah enter his house and then I stood outside in the shadows. That's what happened; that's all that happened. That's how this story really ends. When it comes to what truly matters, the rest of what I've written here is only decorative. At the time, I told myself I stood so still because I thought it wise to behave as a respectable, responsible citizen. Leave justice to the system in place. Enough lives had already been thrown into turmoil. There was no way for me to untrouble them and nothing to gain in troubling them further. I thought of myself as a man of restraint, and with that thought I stepped out of the shelter and set off into the night. But I'd hardly reached the nearest corner before I saw that my restraint was really only a retreat into my habitual state of doing nothing at all.

I stopped at the end of Noah's street. I didn't care that the rain fell on me in a torrent. I felt a groundswell of disgust, disgust from deep in my bones, for having so long lived like such a coward, for having swallowed my words instead of spitting them in his face. It wasn't true that I'd had no words with which to address Noah's crime. The words had been with me for more than a decade. They'd come to me, if inchoate, as soon as I received the news from Lindsay. I'd kept them all the while, I knew, and now perhaps they were all I had. But still they were raving, disordered, thrashing senselessly in my head, and rather than trying to master them and shepherd them into the world, the truth was that I kept them caged because that was a simpler way of keeping my fury at bay.

Now here they are, and my anger as well, a slew of words gushing out from the blackest, most craven part of myself. Gushing into a safehaven of stillness and silence, flooding across the desert of the empty page. I turned the corner and, looking back, I watched Noah's house escape my sight. The rain lashed my face and soaked through my clothes as I pressed on towards the city. Lives I might have changed forever continued to unfold as if I didn't even exist. I took my punishment in the cold, with rising gorge and the scald of rancour on my tongue, and as I set off I searched for words to cleanse me of the fire I couldn't contain anymore.

SPLICE

ThisIsSplice.co.uk